Mia's Nutcracker Ballet

By Robin Farley • Pictures by Olga and Aleksey Ivanov

HARPER

An Imprint of HarperCollinsPublishers

*For little ballerinas
Lydia and Mila
—A. and O. I.*

Copyright © 2013 by HarperCollins Publishers
All rights reserved. Manufactured in China.
No part of this book may be used or reproduced in any manner whatsoever without written permission except in the case of brief quotations embodied in critical articles and reviews.
For information address HarperCollins Children's Books, a division of HarperCollins Publishers, 10 East 53rd Street, New York, NY 10022.
www.harpercollinschildrens.com
Library of Congress catalog card number: 2012955956
ISBN 978-0-06-223830-6
Graphic design by Sean Boggs
13 14 15 16 17   SCP   10 9 8 7 6 5 4 3 2 1
❖
First Edition

On a cold winter's night from inside her cozy room,
Mia watches a special ballet outside her window.
The sky hangs like a dark curtain.
The moon shines like a spotlight.
And snowflakes dance like tiny ballerinas,
swaying and twirling in the wind.

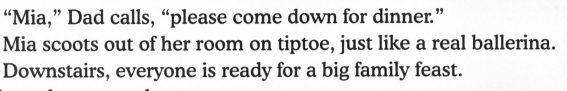

"Mia," Dad calls, "please come down for dinner."
Mia scoots out of her room on tiptoe, just like a real ballerina.
Downstairs, everyone is ready for a big family feast.
Mia makes a grand entrance.
"Watch this!" she says, spinning her finest pirouette.

Mia's big sister giggles. "I taught her that," says Ava.
Ava is a ballerina. Mia wants to be just like her when she grows up.

After dessert it is time for presents. Grandpa saves his gift for last:
a bright red box with gold and silver bows.

"This is for our littlest dancer," he says with a smile.

Mia opens the box. Inside is a wooden toy. It looks like a man in a suit.
When Mia moves the back of his coat, his mouth opens and closes.

"A nutcracker!" says Ava. She is very excited. But Mia does not understand.

"Do you know the story of the *Nutcracker* ballet?" asks Grandpa.
Mia shakes her head.

"Come here and I will tell you," he says. "It starts on a night just like this one. . . ."
Mia closes her eyes and listens very, very carefully.

One Christmas eve, a little girl named Clara is at a fancy party. There are lots of people. There are lots of presents. Clara and her brother, Fritz, help decorate the beautiful tree.

Suddenly, the door opens. Clara's godfather has come to join them, bringing gifts for all the boys and girls. He has a special present just for Clara: a small wooden nutcracker.

The other children laugh when they see Clara's present.
Fritz thinks it's so silly that he throws it on the ground.
He breaks the nutcracker's jaw!

But little Clara loves her toy. She cradles the nutcracker and wraps a bandage around his head. She rocks him to sleep and lays him down to rest. Then Clara goes to bed, too.

Later, Clara slips out of bed to visit the nutcracker. She tiptoes over just as
the clock strikes twelve. When the last chime sounds,
something strange starts to happen.

The Christmas tree grows bigger and bigger. . . .
The whole room becomes enormous!
Little gray mice creep out of every corner, including one Mouse King,
much bigger than the others. . . .

Clara clutches her toy by the hand.
"Please protect me," she whispers.
"I will," says the nutcracker.
Clara can't believe her ears.

The nutcracker has come to life!

The nutcracker springs into action. He tells the Mouse King to leave at once, but the Mouse King just laughs. The two start to fight, dancing faster and faster. Clara worries that her friend will get hurt! She knows she must help him stop the Mouse King.

In a flash, Clara makes a decision. She takes off her shoe and throws it with all her might at the Mouse King. He is so surprised that he runs away immediately!

"I guess we protect each other," says a voice.
Clara turns around and gasps.
First the nutcracker had come to life. And
now he had turned into a handsome prince!

You have been so kind to me," the prince says to Clara. "You cared for me when everyone laughed. You helped me scare away the Mouse King. I want to thank you with something special."

The prince leads Clara outside. With a wave of his hand, the snowflakes falling to the ground come to life. They dance and sing for Clara.

"Please come with me to my kingdom," says the prince.
"My friend the Sugar Plum Fairy will want to meet you."
The prince helps Clara into a boat. There are dolphins in the water,
waiting to take them wherever they want to go.
"To the Land of Sweets," the prince says.

Clara watches the Land of Sweets get closer with every swish
of the dolphins' tails. Soon, she can see the whole kingdom.
There are candy-cane houses. There are gumdrops on every corner.
The snow covers everything like frosting on a cupcake.
Clara has never seen anything quite so beautiful.

The Sugar Plum Fairy curtsies as she greets the prince and Clara.
"We've heard all about your kindness and your bravery," she tells Clara.
"Tonight, you are our guest of honor!"

One by one, the people of
the kingdom dance for Clara.
First comes the chocolate dance . . .

then the coffee dance . . .

and the tea dance . . .

and a waltz performed
by delicate flowers.

Finally, the Sugar Plum Fairy dances a very special ballet. She glides. She twirls. She leaps high in the air. Her toe shoes move so swiftly that Clara gasps in wonder.

"Thank you, Clara, for all that you have done!" the people of the Land of Sweets call. "Please stay with us forever."

The Sugar Plum Fairy puts a crown on Clara's head. The prince takes her hand.

"Hooray for Clara, our hero!" they sing.

The Land of Sweets is loud with cheers.

"And that is the story of the *Nutcracker* ballet," says Grandpa. "What do you think, Mia?"

Mia is quiet. She is still imagining the Sugar Plum Fairy's dance.

"I think it's time for bed, little one," says Mom.

Mom helps Mia up to her room. She gives Mia a kiss.
Mia snuggles under the covers. Her very own nutcracker is keeping watch
by her bed.

"We'll always protect each other," she whispers as she drifts off to sleep.

Outside her window, the snowflakes dance their special ballet. They twirl and sway in the wind, covering Mia's house in a thin layer of frosting—just like they did in the Land of Sweets.